The Crows That Ate Sunday

Daz Eek

Note From Author

Please note, as an English author, it's only natural for me to use UK spellings rather than those of American English, like 'colour' instead of 'color', for example. I hope you enjoy the story!

Join Daz Eek's newsletter for news on future book releases at https://dazeek.blog/.

For Theo

Contents

Archibald

The Reverend Archibald Oxley had to admire the creature's persistence; from the cross to peck at the window, from the window to rest atop the cross, the crow flew, over and over, as regular as clockwork, tick-tock.

Archibald, with all the bodily virtues one would expect of a village vicar, sat at his desk without a Christmas Day sermon written. The crow wouldn't allow it. He looked out of the vestry's lancet window to the crow, watching him intently from the cross that marked the last resting place of the church's greatest benefactor, Sir Lionel Orton. Even in that moment of dawn, when one thing could still look like quite another, he recognized the crow. What would come of it he didn't know, but it had come to this and there was to be no shying away. He'd the eyes to see.

Archibald sighed with annoyance. The crow. The diocese's letter. It wouldn't do. He wouldn't do, drunk as he was. He should've waited to open the last of the wine until after the service. They'd be with him soon enough. Those that still came. They'd expect their Christmas Word, or they too would go with the rest of them. What good was a vicar without parishioners? That was the gist of the diocese's letter.

He looked down at the blank piece of paper in front of him without a good or bad word within him to put down on it.

"Here crow, have this," Archibald said, and with that he took aim and tossed an empty wine bottle at the crow peck-pecking the window. Immediately, he regretted his outburst as while the bottle striking the window had frightened the crow back to its perch above the venerable Sir Lionel Orton, it had also broken the window so that a large spider web crack of glass was now visible with a hole in the middle where the spider might sit. Soon enough, for the sake of a spider, the crow returned to the window and, with calm detachment, began extracting shards of red and green glass with its beak.

"Let it be easier for it, I don't care," Archibald said, and he sucked up a final bead of wine from the communion chalice he'd borrowed for his Christmas morning drinking. He'd said to himself that he'd never go back to the horrid place. Now he'd have to.

"This must be some Christmas party, Archie!" the man at the off-licence had said.

Archibald hadn't known the man from Adam, but the man had taken it upon himself to know him well enough to butcher his name without compunction. His name was Archibald. Not Archie. He loathed the diminutive of the name his mother had chosen for him. His father had called him Archie.

The man introduced himself as Frank and then motored into conversation with a lane wide enough for only the one participant. "I know I've never been up to yours, but I don't get along with God. Your predecessor knew that well enough. May he rest in peace," he said. "A Christmas party, you say? Now there's a turn up."

Archibald knew on the spot that Frank believed his reason for buying the wine was a ruse. He'd the eyes to see. He'd lied when the police had visited him, and the police never knew when he'd lied. Frank, though, knew his lie.

With Frank holding the wine hostage, Archibald, of course, had no recourse but to submit himself to more of the shopkeeper's interminable babble which, much to his discomfort, was about the man he'd replaced at St Michael's. Frank said that he'd never have taken the old vicar for a vicar in a month of Sundays, and that was what he had called him—the old vicar. There'd been a reverence in all the letters that made up all the words when he said it, a reverence that was not in the words that Frank used for him. His name wasn't Archie. He was the Reverend Archibald Oxley.

The old vicar was a regular, Frank said, coming in every Wednesday evening for a chat and a packet of cheese and onion crisps. If Frank was running low on cheese and onion crisps, he'd set aside a bag or two for the old vicar especially, because that's what the old vicar always bought, regular as clockwork, tick-tock. Not wine. Cheese and onion crisps. Then Frank said that he'd split his sides while listening to the old vicar's funny stories about the goings-on of living a religious life. If ever there was someone who was going to stick his bum to a pew, Frank said, it would've been the old vicar with the glue to do it.

Frank ended their meeting by handing over the case of wine, saying how horrible it was that the old vicar's time should've ended the way it did, adding for effect—but you can't believe all that you hear, can you? Archibald understood what Frank was getting at. He didn't need a picture drawn. The entire village was the same. How dare they believe differently from the police! What right did they have? How he'd seen them run!

"How do you do, Mrs Williams? Will I see you at church this Sunday?" he'd asked, and Mrs Williams had looked straight through him as though he were a windowpane with nothing to see on the other side.

"Nice to see you out on a day as cold as this, Mr Lewis. It's cold up at the church, but we can turn up the central heating if the collection permits this Sunday," he'd said, and Mr Lewis had slunk into the warmth of a pub without so much as a by-your-leave, saying as he went something to everyone inside that had brought on uproarious laughter.

"May I say again, Mrs Johnston, how sorry I am about your husband's passing. I hope you liked the service," he'd said. "I see you putting the flowers down every Friday. You can always come in, you know, for a cup of tea after." Mrs Johnston had then taken it upon herself to dash across the road, gesturing at the butcher's shop window sign for fifty-pence off of a pound of bacon. The number seven bus had all but run her over.

Archibald sprung up from his desk with the energy of a Jack free from its box. "To hell with them all! This is my church, and they won't take it away from me!"

The crow flew back to the broken window, regular as clockwork, tick-tock, peck-peck, crack-crack.

"Come in crow, come in. We can see each other again if that's what you'd like," Archibald said. "Then I'll see to the others." He then wobbled from the vestry with thoughts of the communion wine that was his for the taking, and which for the rest of the day at least would do in a pinch.

Alex

Alex woke from a deathly dream bleeding into reality. There, weighing down the edge of his bed, was his father, Jack, a thick slab of meat.

"Off with your church tart?" Jack asked.

Alex pushed himself away from his father, up against the headboard of his bed, an uncomfortable mess of teenage bones. He knew his father wanted a fight. He'd heard the punches his father wanted to throw in his voice. It was all to do with the backpack his father held.

"I asked you a question," Jack said.

Alex couldn't find the words to answer his father. Those had run away deep within him, playing hide and seek. He watched his father unzip the backpack and then look inside with his eyes and then his hands. Inside of the backpack were all the possessions that meant the most to him, those he'd wanted to take. He was in there, and now his father was in there with him. He didn't want his father in there with him.

Alex watched his father chuck clothes and books and music from out of the backpack and onto the bedroom carpet. He and Jill were going, but now his father was inside of his backpack, and they wouldn't be going. Jill had said it didn't matter where they'd go. There was a train to take them anywhere and things would be better there. They'd be together, he'd see. Now he wouldn't see. It now all seemed such a silly idea. That wasn't real life, real life was here with his father.

Jack stood up from the bed, the now empty backpack hanging limp from a tree burl fist like a hung man. "Jill's her name, right?" Jack asked.

Alex hated the name of her coming out of his father's body.

"I'll tell you what," Jack said. "If you can show me how much you want to run off with your church tart, I'll think about letting you go. It'll be my Christmas present to you."

Alex watched his father drop the rucksack and roll up his shirt sleeves.

"You may as well have a go," Jack said, beckoning Alex forward with his fighter's hands. "It's happening whether or not you like it."

Alex lifted the bedcovers.

Crow

The others did not know it was here.
They were nothing in the high places.
They could not see.
When the light came.
They would be something.
They would see.
It should not be here.
This was not their way.
It knew the long bone.

Jill

Jill stood outside of the closed chip shop as though it were both the first and the last place she wanted to be that Sunday morning. Alex was late. Where was he? They should've been on their way to the train station by now, together. They would've had a good start on their families, and it would've been too late for them to catch up even if they knew where they were going.

Jill couldn't help thinking something had gone wrong, and that Alex wasn't coming. But she also knew that Alex was never on time for anything. She'd joked with him in the past about how he'd probably be late for his own funeral. He'd even been late for their first date. Back then, she'd almost walked away from outside of the same chip shop, giving Alex up for good and thinking to herself how he'd blown his chance with her forever. Then down the road came Alex, running, a tangle of arms and legs every which way, shouting: "Wait, don't go! I'm here! Sorry!" She again looked up the road, but this time there was no Alex, only an old, tall man wearing a long coat and hat approaching her; even from a distance, he seemed impossibly tall.

It was early enough in the morning that Jill hadn't expected to see another person except for Alex. Should she call him? No. She knew Alex's home situation well enough. She may end up with his father on the other end. Maybe Alex's father had found out about their plans? That was her, a born worrier. She looked at her watch. Soon her family would want her to get up, shouting up at her from downstairs that it was time for breakfast, church.

Jill watched as the old, tall man came closer, his loping stride eating up the pavement. He seemed harmless enough, didn't he? Still, here she was, a girl alone, with no one else around, and the old, tall man getting closer and closer. If this had been her first date with Alex, she would've left ages ago. She wouldn't have stood around waiting for him this amount of time back then. Now, though, it was different. She'd probably wait around for Alex until, what? The end of time? The chip shop opened? That last moment she could safely escape the old, tall man?

Out of the corner of her eye, Jill caught a movement from inside of the chip shop. She turned to see that it was Christos, the owner of the chip shop, up early, readying for opening time. Christos waved at her and then pointed to his watch to say they weren't open yet. She waved back and mouthed the words she was waiting for someone. Christos seemed to understand her and disappeared into the back of the chip shop. Christos really made the best chips in the whole of Birmingham. She'd miss coming here with Alex for their usual. For her it was chips with extra salt and vinegar and a pickled egg. For Alex it was chips and curry sauce. It's what they'd ordered the afternoon she'd waited for Alex, their first date. It's what they ordered each time they met at the chip shop after. Alex always bought her the pickled egg. Sometimes he went without curry sauce just so she could have the pickled egg. Christos and his brothers always tried to encourage them to order a battered cod or a chicken and mushroom pie, saying they'd say they'd never become millionaires if the two of them only ever ordered a pickled egg and curry sauce with their chips.

A hand tapped Jill on her shoulder. She turned, lit up inside. "Alex!"

It wasn't Alex.

Jill saw that old, tall man was even taller now, standing right next to her. She looked up into his eyes, eyes that were looking down upon her. Maybe he wasn't that tall? She was small, after all. Most people were taller than her. Alex was taller than her by a foot, but with the old, tall man, she may as well have been standing next to a lamppost.

"I know an Alex," the old, tall man said. "He's up at the church."

"My Alex?" Jill asked.

The tall man laughed. "No, it couldn't be your Alex. Not unless he's seventy-one and six-feet under."

The old, tall man bent over Jill and squeezed his eyes as though he was a microscope and Jill was a blot for closer studying. "I know you, don't I?"

Jill was sure she'd never met her inquisitor before. "I don't think so." She looked past the old, tall man to see if Alex was on his way, but he wasn't there.

The old, tall man snapped his fingers. "That's right, you're a Church One."

"A what?" Jill said.

"A Church One. You go where I work, to St Michael's up the road. I've seen you, right? With your family. Your mom and dad, and the little girl, your sister, yes?"

It unnerved Jill to have a stranger know so much about her.

The old, tall man smiled. "You don't know me, do you? Few of you do up there. I'm not a Church One, you see. I just tend the grounds, dig the graves, do other odd jobs here and there. Keeps me busy."

It was then that Jill vaguely recognised the old, tall man. That was if he were to take off his hat, which resembled a chimney pot. "Yes, I've seen you," she said. "Sorry, I'm not very good with faces."

"Oh, I am," said the old, tall man. "I know all the Church Ones. I see them come and go. More gone than seen nowadays, mind you."

"My name's Jill," Jill said, just so she could stop being called a Church One.

"Pleased to meet you, Jill," said the old, tall man. "My name's Ernie."

Ernie put out his hand to shake.

Jill took Ernie's hand in hers and it felt like holding hands with Winter. "Pleased to meet you."

"No, you're not," Ernie said. "You wanted to see this Alex, not me. Is he a Church One too?"

"Yes, he's a Church One," Jill said. "I mean, yes, he goes to church."

"Then I know the boy you mean. He's the one you look at when you think no one else is looking at you looking at him."

Jill blushed. "I don't know what you're talking about."

"Don't worry, I won't say anything to anyone. I just see the stories all. If you've got eyes in your head, you can see the stories if you want to see them. Better than the tele it is."

Out of habit now, Jill looked at her watch.

"What if he doesn't come?" Ernie asked.

"He'll be here, not that it's any of your business," Jill said.

"It isn't my business. I'm just able to see the stories going on. Put two and two together, if you like. I'm not trying to frighten you."

"What do you mean, frighten me?"

"Oh, nothing."

"Tell me."

"Alex will do that. Up at the church. You'll see."

A chill lept into Jill's body. There was something in the way Ernie talked about Alex not coming to meet her, but being at church, which was so casually easy, as though it was the whole truth and nothing but the truth.

This time it was Ernie's turn to see the hour of the day. "Look at that. I was late already and now I'm later."

Ernie walked on, leaving Jill alone, shouting as he went. "Nice meeting you, Jill! Bundle up! The snow will be here soon!"

Jill stamped her feet and held herself tightly to warm herself up against the iciness that Ernie had placed inside of her.

Archibald

Archibald sat on the church chancel's stone steps, halfway into the communion wine, listening to the crow making a god-awful racket inside of the church.

"Well done, birdie, you found your way in!" Archibald said.

Archibald slugged his wine. If only the diocese could see how he was handling the situation with the crow, they'd have no recourse but to apologise for having sent him the letter. Of course, knowing them, they'd mark it down to being an administrative error, saying they'd fired the person responsible after some well-chosen, stern words. Yes, you'll never hear from that individual again, they'd say, and you certainly won't hear from us. Keep up the good work!

Archibald wondered if he should make it harder for the crow to find him? Play a game of hide and seek? He let go of the idea quickly. He'd drunk too much wine for horseplay, or crow play as it were. Rather, he'd wait where he was beneath Christ crucified. Besides, he didn't want to worry the sermon that was taking shape inside of his head, words stringing together, all of them making perfect sense. It would be a sermon for the ages. Pleased with himself, he stood to dance a jig of glee down the chancel's stone steps, hoisting the wine bottle into the air as though it were a trophy he'd won. "Come, my crow! Come, my flock! I'm waiting for you!"

Archibald halted his dance at the sound of breaking glass. Was that the crow free of the vestry, knocking down the framed photo of Bishop Mortimer and him, all smiles? How the day was turning around for the better! He'd only hung the photo in the first place so that it would impress people. Not that anybody had been. What a sad sack of bones Bishop Mortimer was. It was he who should be a Bishop, not the old porridge face. When the Bishop had visited, it had been all words of grief and blessed remembrance for the old vicar, and not a single word of congratulations or encouragement for his appointment. If the opportunity ever presented itself, he'd take care of the Bishop.

Archibald found himself caught on a wave of wine breaking throughout him, sloshing the words of his sermon about so that they formed new sentences, a new sermon, a better sermon. All of a wobble, he looked up at Christ hanging on his cross, pointing to the statue and then to himself. "You and me," he said, "you and me."

On this, Archibald wrapped his arms around the Christ statue and if anyone were to have seen the spectacle, they might've thought that Archibald had become part of the statue himself. "You'll look after me, won't you? I've tried in my own way to look after you. They're all trying to take it away from me. If you spoke to me, helped me, they'd have to listen. A few words would do. One word even. Anything. Can you spare the time for me?"

Archibald finished the communion wine, dribbles of it falling from his lips and down his chin and onto his white clergy collar, streaking it a bloody red. He broke away from the Christ statue. "Say something!"

In response to hearing nothing, nothing but the crow, louder and louder, Archibald flung the wine bottle at the Christ statue. The bottle broke into pieces, and so did Christ's nose. He laughed, a laugh of a man knocking on the door of insanity. He then approached the Christ statue and took hold of it. At first the statue wouldn't budge, but then it did for him, and then it did some more, and then it was wobbling back and forth like it too had been drinking wine all Sunday morning long. He wasn't a vigorous man, but he was vigorous with spirit. With Spirit, his flock would return to him. With Spirit, he would put an end to the crow that wanted to put an end to him.

"I know what I do," Archibald said, and with that he shoved the Christ statue to the stone floor and watched with great satisfaction as the statue smashed into pieces, Christ's head rolling away to disappear under a pew. What followed was the crow, strutting among broken feet and hands and arms and legs, making enough noise to raise heaven and hell, if he hadn't done so already. The crow cocked its head to the side and laid a black, beady eye on him. For a greeting, he coughed up a piece of drunk sickness inside of him and spat it at his visitor. He missed with his so that the red and green gob of putridness was, instead, caught by one of the Christ statue's hands. The crow took flight into the church's high places with much to say about matters.

Jack

"Is he all right?"

Jack had looked out of his front lounge window to make sure the nosey old bag wasn't around, and he hadn't seen hide nor hair of her. He should've known better that Gertrude, his neighbour, would pop her candy-floss, permed head above the hedgerow that separated their houses.

"He's fine," Jack said, nearly to the car, keeping a half-conscious Alex upright as best he could.

"Doesn't look fine to me," Gertrude said, peering over the hedgerow, trying to get a better look. "What happened to the poor lad?"

"Nothing for you to worry about." Jack had long wished Gertrude would drop dead. She was past the age for it to happen. Still, she'd kept on living. There'd been many times he'd thought about speeding along the process with his own hands. He'd actually planted some foxglove in the back garden with the mind to one day harvesting the poisonous petals for some kind of salad that he'd one day take around to her under the pretence of a peace offering.

Jack propped Alex up against the car. The boy was coming around, but not so much as to cause a scene. The sooner he could get Alex into the car without a word from him for Gertrude to hear, the better.

"Taking him to the hospital?" Gertrude asked.

"Church," Jack said.

"Church, in that state? No, it's a doctor that should look down on him, not God. I was a carer once, for a short while, but I still remember a lot of what to do. If you like, I can have a look at him just to make sure he's all right."

"He's good enough for church." Jack opened the car's backseat door and wrestled Alex inside of the car. He slammed the door shut on Alex and walked to the other side of the car.

"Rather him than me, then. I was there for the old vicar. But I'm not for the new one. Did the old vicar ever pack them in! If he'd sold tickets, he would've been a rich man. You could've heard that church of a Sunday over in Coventry, I bet, and those in Coventry would've had to say why they must have something going on over in Birmingham! Not anymore though, but you'd know that going up there. No, it's not like it used to be. It's such a pity the old vicar had to die like that."

Jack opened the driver's door. "I wish you'd die like that."

"What's that you say?" Gertude asked.

"I said, I like the new vicar."

"Don't tell me you haven't heard? It was in all the papers and not just the local ones, either. It was even on the tele."

"There's no TV in my house."

"No TV? You don't want to watch what's on?"

"I watch my Alex."

"I see."

Jack shut the driver's door. What was that tone in his neighbour's voice just then? He clenched the car keys in his hand so that they dug into his flesh and pressed against bone. Putting on a smile that would've looked fine on a fox approaching a chicken, he walked over to Gertrude, to face her at the hedgerow. "What do you see?"

"It's only every time I see the lad, he's looking behind him, like someone is after him, you know," Gertrude said. "Which is why I bring it up, you saying you watch him and all. Alex is his name, yes? But never mind me, I've a right mouth on me when I get going, always have, always will. Probably put away my Harry, it did."

Jack had done it before he even thought about doing it. If the hedgerow had been higher, he wouldn't have been able to. He walked back to the car. There would be no shying away from the day now. What he'd done wouldn't allow for that. He may as well make the best of things, not that he wasn't enjoying himself already. It was Christmas, after all.

Vivian

A scream simmered inside of Vivian as she stood at the foot of the stairs, bundled up in woollen knits. "Your breakfast is on the table and it's getting cold. Hurry down, Jill, please!"

Vivian despaired about her eldest. It was as though Jill had become a stranger to her over the past six months. Sometimes she even felt like Jill wasn't at home, even when she knew she was at home. She walked back into the kitchen and there, laid out before her, was her Christmas morning breakfast table tableau: Robert wrapped up in his newspaper and Martha, eyes as bright and then dark as two blinking fairy lights, drawing in her pad, her box of colouring pencils all worn to the nub. She was glad there was a fresh box to be found under the tree after church. Absent was Jill. Vivian touched an emptiness inside of her chest that Jill could only fill, sitting at the breakfast table with the rest of her family.

Vivian sighed. Jill would be off to university next year, a London one if all went well, not the Birmingham one. That was Jill's plan. There'd be an empty seat at the breakfast table seven days of the week then. What would she do? No, she didn't want to think about that too much. She wanted to have a pleasant Christmas Day, a day to remember fondly. Jill hadn't gone yet. She'd go upstairs and see what was keeping Jill. She couldn't hear any movement from her daughter, not in her bedroom, not walking along the upstairs landing to the bathroom, not trudging down the stairs. A thought came to her that Jill was sick in bed and incapable of calling out for help. All the times she'd cared for Jill when she'd been ill in that bed! Mumps, measles, chicken pox, the flu, there was a time when if there was something to catch Jill would catch it, regular as clockwork, tick-tock.

"I'll go up and see what's going on," Vivian said.

From behind his newspaper, Robert said, "She'll be here. Any more tea in the pot?"

Vivian bit her nails, a bad habit that presented itself whenever she was anxious. She shoved the offending hand inside of her cardigan pocket where it tinkered with a hanky and cough drops. She couldn't stand for her family, let alone other people, to see her as less than put together. It was important to her to be seen as a person who could weather any storm, even when inside she felt like a wind could easily blow her away to distant parts. She supposed she got that from her mother.

"Never mind," Robert said. "I've had three cups already. I'll be wanting the loo by the time we're singing the first hymn. You know how I get caught short sometimes."

"Robert, please. Not at the breakfast table." Vivian said.

"Yes, dear."

Vivian paced around the breakfast table. "I was looking forward to that drive in the country before church today. The four of us. We always used to go for a drive before church."

"We could skip church."

"Not on Christmas Day."

"Lots are."

"That doesn't mean we have to."

"Yes, dear."

Vivian continued her laps of the breakfast table. She couldn't stop herself. Until, that was, she came upon Martha and saw what her youngest had drawn and was now frantically colouring with a black pencil. She came to a full stop. "Time to put your pencils away now, Martha," she said. "We've got to get ready for church."

Martha looked up at Vivian with eyes that were as black as the black from out of her colouring pencil. "I haven't finished Uncle Crow. Anyway, Jill isn't here. I can keep on longer."

"She'll be here," Robert said.

"Who's Uncle Crow?" Vivian asked.

"He's new," Martha said.

Vivian remembered when Martha used to draw nothing but flowers. Now it was Uncle Crow. She didn't like the look of Uncle Crow at all. "Why didn't you draw Uncle Bob instead?" Vivian asked.

Robert huffed from behind his newspaper.

"Who's Uncle Bob?" Martha asked, carrying on colouring.

"Oh, I want to give up, I really do," Vivian said, going back to her laps around the breakfast table. "You all knew I wanted to go for a Christmas drive before church today. We spoke about it last Sunday. We could've been together, a family."

"We're a family now," Robert said.

"Not without Jill," Vivian said.

"She'll be here," Robert said.

Vivian passed the setting laid out for Jill, her scrambled egg and buttered toast untouched on her plate, a breakfast that used to be her favourite. Jill used to hurry down from upstairs to fill up on scrambled eggs and buttered toast, but not anymore. "Her breakfast is stone cold."

"Jill doesn't eat scrambled eggs anymore," Martha said, colouring away, "only pickled eggs."

"I like pickled eggs," Robert said.

"I've never had a pickled egg," Martha said.

Robert turned a page of his newspaper. "You'd like them."

"Jill likes them," Martha said.

"They're a real treat." Robert said.

"Why are you all suddenly talking about pickled eggs? Stop it!" Vivian said.

Robert ruffled his newspaper so that the pages fell in front of him straight. "When you're at the shops next, dear, can you see about picking some up for us?" Robert asked.

"Jill shouldn't be the only one to have pickled eggs," Martha said.

"Pickled eggs all around, dear," Robert said.

"There'll be no pickled eggs in this house, ever," Vivian said.

"Dad, what's wrong with Mom?" Martha asked, finishing up her colouring. "Why can't we have pickled eggs when Jill does?"

"Mom's just fine, dear. No need to worry," Robert said.

Vivian circled the breakfast table faster and faster, her slippers flap-flapping over the linoleum floor. "I'm not fine! If you looked up from that newspaper of yours once in a while, you'd see that for yourself!"

Vivian looked up at the kitchen ceiling, beyond which was Jill's bedroom. "Jill! Get yourself down those stairs now or heaven help me I'll come up there and drag you down myself!"

As if on cue, Jill walked into the kitchen through the kitchen door that led out to the back garden.

Vivian stopped her pacing around the kitchen table and stared at her daughter. "Where have you been? I've been calling you down for ages like a silly fool."

"Just out for a walk," Jill said.

"Mom is going to buy us all pickled eggs," Martha said. "Just like the ones you like to eat, Jill."

Jill gave Martha a look. "What?"

"So then, are we all ready for church?" Robert asked, closing and folding his newspaper.

"I am," Martha said, triumphantly holding up her completed drawing. "Uncle Crow's coming too!"

Vivian looked at everyone, back together again, her family. As she had done countless times before, she didn't let out the scream inside of her that was past a simmer to a boil, splutter and splatter.

Crow

A long time ago.

We followed the long bones into their wars.

We feasted.

We knew the taste of a long bone.

Fallen.

The taste is a memory.

Passed on down.

Within us.

From those that are now nothing.

This long bone.

Has not fallen.

This long bone tastes different.

Warm.

It would tell the others.

Archibald

Archibald watched the crow fly up into the rafters of the church where it settled, tasting his blood as though it were having a conversation with it. He gestured at the crow in a way that would've given the Archbishop conniptions. "It's you who are beneath me!"

His words fell out of him in a drunken slur. The blasted bird had given him far more trouble than he'd expected. For every blow that he'd struck, the crow had reciprocated in kind. At stages of the battle, particularly when the crow had been about his ear, he'd wondered that if he were to lose, would they give him a good burial, one rightfully fitting of his position? No, he'd decided bitterly, it would be a rushed affair without ceremony and with no one in attendance. Ernie certainly wouldn't be in too much of a hurry to dig his grave. The old codger would most likely dig him back up on the sly and then open up his coffin for crows miles around to feast on his remains.

Archibald shook a blood-streaked fist at the crow as it, suitably rested, it seemed, swooped down from on high to circle him, an almighty racket of caws. "Come and get some of this!"

The crow for its part took Archibald up on the suggestion and dipped and lifted and dipped and lifted so that he, clumsy through inebriation, could never quite touch a finger to feather. They were shenanigans that opened up another door of madness within Archibald, one that he gladly walked through to see what was there and what would be of use to him. "Play with me, would you, crow? I'll teach you about playing when I get a hold of you, and I'll take great pleasure in it!"

Of course, the crow in its own way was becoming as clumsy as Archibald, drunk not on wine, but with plain tiredness. Out of sheer luck, arms and hands flailing, Archibald caught hold of the crow and let out a cry of manic satisfaction. The crow pecked wildly at Archibald's hand, pulling flesh away in ribbon strips. Through all the pain subjected upon him by the flapping and cacophonous crow, Archibald persevered in holding onto his prize. He'd see the crow make his hand useless for the rest of his life before he'd let go. He had to commend the crow. His predecessor hadn't put up this kind of fight. He'd fallen quick enough to take all the satisfaction out of the killing. On another day, perhaps, a better day, perhaps, he wouldn't have thrown the stone at the crow. The letter from the diocese had woken up such an anger in him he had to find a place to put it. That place had been with the crow.

Archibald flung the crow to the church's stone floor. He fancied he heard more of the crow's tiny bones break. He stood over the crow triumphantly. The crow looked up at him with what was something like hatred, but what did he care about a common bird's feelings for him? He kicked the crow a few feet down the church's aisle, taking quiet delight in how the crow's pain sang through the church as loud as an organ playing the most god-fearing Sunday hymn. How the old vicar had sounded much the same way! Now how would he finish the crow?

Archibald knelt down in front of the crow, now flopping around in an ever-decreasing circle. The other week, he'd seen what used to be one of the old vicar's regulars, Mrs Lassiter was her name, dropped in the street while she was out shopping, all of her potatoes out of her carrier and rolling away from her into the gutter. She'd flopped about just like the crow, as though her arms and legs were being pulled by invisible puppeteer strings. He'd walked away from her, as she'd walked away from him.

An idea came to Archibald, one that lit up his face like a flame atop a burning candle. From out of his trouser pocket, he pulled a silver crucifix on a long silver chain. Then, around and around and around, he set about wrapping the chain of the crucifix about the crow's neck until it shut up for good and fell still and he'd restored peace to the church once more.

Derek and Carol

"Let's not go," Derek said, helping Carol into her new overcoat, picking off a bit of snowman wrapping paper stuck to it with tape. "Why don't we binge watch that new show you were talking about?"

"It's good for me and the baby to get out," Carol said. "Besides, if I have to stay another day cooped up in this house, I might come at you with the kitchen knife later. I wouldn't be to blame. I'd tell the jury it was my hormones that did it, not me."

"Did I say that while we were binge watching the show, I'd be rubbing your feet, just the way you like."

"About that."

"What?"

"I don't like the way you rub my feet."

"Don't you?"

"You know those people who say aliens have experimented on them?"

"You're not saying?"

"I am."

"Why didn't you tell me sooner?"

"You seemed to have so much fun."

"But you weren't?"

"No."

Derek lifted his hands for closer examination. "I've alien hands?"

"Only in the foot-rubbing department," Carol said, buttoning up her overcoat.

"All those foot rubs I've been giving you, trying to be a good husband, and there you were feeling like you were being subjected to terrible alien experiments," Derek said.

"You're a good husband," Carol said. "You're taking me to church today. Of course, I can go by myself."

"I wouldn't be able to rest knowing you were there, and I was here."

"I'm a big girl, you know."

"Getting bigger by the day."

Carrie slapped Derek across the shoulder. "Less of that."

Derek made like he was a hypnotist. "You're under my spell. You'll do as I say. You don't want to go to church. You want to stay at home with me. Repeat after me: church is no fun, church is no fun, church is no fun. My alien hands command you!"

"You're ridiculous," Carol said, "now let's go now so we can get a good seat up front. I want the vicar to have a good impression of us before we ask him about the christening."

"I wasn't christened, and I turned out fine," Derek said.

"Some would say," Carol said, opening the front door and walking outside.

Derek grabbed his overcoat from off the hallway hat and coat rack and rushed after Carol, locking the front door to the house on the way out. "Charming! Remind me again why you ever bothered with me?"

"That's what my mother keeps asking," Carol said, walking past their car in the driveway.

Derek put his hand on the car. "Where are you off to?"

"We're walking," Carol said, "it's only up the road."

Derek caught up with Carol and grabbed her arm. "They said it was going to snow on the radio."

"Come on, fuss pot," Carol said, pulling Derek along with her. "The walk will do you some good, too. I'm not the only one to have put on a few pounds. Tell me, where did the Stilton go? The Brie? The Cotswold?"

Derek took Carol's hand and guided her down the driveway and onto the pavement, on the way to church, its spire peaking above the trees in the short distance. "You know me and cheese."

"Your bit on the side," Carol said.

"Don't tell the vicar, your christening wouldn't get a look in."

"It's all going to be okay, isn't it?"

"What do you mean?"

"There's been so many changes all at once: the baby, your job, moving. I know you don't like my mother and, heaven help me, I've had my moments with her, but all the same, I miss her. I haven't made a new friend since we came here."

"Perhaps you'll meet a new friend today," Derek said, squeezing Carol's hand, "now watch out for this bit coming up, it may be black ice."

Together, they sidestepped a slip and a fall.

"That noise." Derek said.

"Oh, it's just crows," Carol said.

Derek looked ahead of him and upwards, higher than the church's spire, and there he did indeed see crows, so many loud and back & forth specks of black in the whitening winter sky. "Aren't we supposed to be hearing church bells?"

Alex

From the backseat of the car, Alex willed the traffic light to turn. The traffic light turned as if on his command, green to amber to red. His father slowed down the car, and they came to a stop. Then Alex, groggy from his father's beating, let himself out of the car, missing a collision with a motorbike that was coming up on the side of the car. The motorbike rider stopped at the red light and turned to shake his fist at Alex.

Alex saw none of it, as by then he was across the road and onto the pavement, running in the direction they had just come. Jill would still wait for him. She knew what he was like, late all the time. As he ran, he wondered where his father was now? Had he got out of the car and was now running after him? Was he waiting for the traffic light to turn to green so that he could double back and give chase that way? He could outrun his father, he was sure of it, but he couldn't outrun a car.

Alex picked up his pace. He'd a lot of practice running through the years, from the kids at school who wanted to beat him up over nothing in particular, from his father who'd wanted to beat him up over nothing in particular too. Clipping along the pavement in a gangly mess, he saw the car that Jill's parents drove coming up the road towards him. He knew in an instant that it was the car as there was no one around these parts that drove a red Mini, new decades ago. Nowadays, the car stood out like a sore thumb compared to all the other cars that shared space with it on the roads. He slowed down and came to a stop, panting. He watched the car drive past him. Sitting in the backseat was Jill, smashed up against her little sister, looking out at him. The look on her face said, this is where I am now. Where were you? Then Jill had gone, and he didn't have the legs on him to run anymore.

A woman pushing a toddler in a pram came up to him. "Are you going to stand there all day? I've got a job to get to, and somewhere to drop this one off before that."

"Sorry," Alex said, stepping aside to let the woman push the pram along.

Alex then saw another car that he recognised, but this car didn't carry on without him. This car pulled up alongside the curb. It was his father's car. Inside, he saw his father looking straight ahead, waiting for him to get inside. He knew what he had to do. Jill and her family were going to church, and now he'd have to go too. He wanted to see Jill, to tell her he was sorry, that there would be another day. Wouldn't there? He got into the back of the car. He expected his father to say something, but they drove on in silence. Soon, they approached the same traffic light where he'd made his escape. This time, though, he wasn't going anywhere. There was no point.

At last, his father spoke. "Don't think I didn't see her too," Jack said. "Now we can both see her together. At church."

Alex took his phone out of his pocket.

His father saw what he was doing in the rear-view mirror. "Put it away."

"I'm calling the police," Alex said. He'd lost count of the times he should've called before, but his father had made it clear what the consequences would be if he had done it, and those consequences were always enough to give him nightmares. It would be different this time. He wouldn't give into the nightmares.

"See that woman and her child crossing the road up there?" Jack asked. "Now what does she think she's doing when there's a perfectly good crossing farther up. See it? She must be in a hurry. Well, I'm in a hurry to get where we're going, for you to put the phone away."

Alex felt the car speed up. "You wouldn't?"

"I would. Then after, we'll both drive into that big truck. See it? I'll make sure I'll do a good job of it too. You'll never see that girl of yours again. You'll see anybody again."

Alex saw that the woman pushing the pram across the road was paying no attention to them. She didn't know what his father was capable of. He did. He'd seen it repeatedly, regular as clockwork, tick-tock.

"There are always consequences," his father said.

Alex flung his phone onto the car's front passenger seat.

With that, Jack brought the car to a screeching halt a few feet in front of the woman and her toddler.

Alex watched the woman approach the car. She slammed her hand down on the bonnet. The car's reverberations ran through his body. The woman then looked at him, not his father. "What the bloody hell do you think you're doing? Can't you see I have a young one here. If the little one wasn't with me, I'd have at you, I swear, but I know your face. I can see it, and if I ever see it again by myself, I'll have at you, mark my words, I'll have at you."

The woman then took hold of the pram and finished crossing the road.

"You grew in a pram like that one," his father said.

Alex remembered being in the pram, looking up at his mother's face with her black hair tied up tightly in a bun, the way she'd always worn it, so that it looked as though she were balancing a lump of coal on her head. It was then that he saw his mother's face appear in the car's rear-view mirror, replacing his father's face. She'd let her hair down, and it was long and flowing and lifting about her face as though she'd sprouted black wings. She'd flown away, leaving him with his father. Then he wasn't seeing his mother's face, he was seeing his father's face again, smiling back at him. There were always consequences.

Martha

For something to do, Martha poked Jill in the ribs. "That was your boyfriend back there," she said.

"Shut up," Jill said, edging away from Martha, but the backseat of a Mini only afforded her so much personal space.

"I saw you both that time. Mom didn't see you. She was driving. But I saw. You were eating a pickled egg, and now we're all going to have pickled eggs. Dad asked Mom to get some."

"I don't know what you're talking about."

"Mom, Dad, I've got something to tell you," Martha said.

"Tell me later," Robert said, "your mom and I are talking."

Martha smiled at Jill. "See, I'll tell them everything. You're not old enough to go anywhere. Not until another year, Mom and Dad said. And when you go, I'm going to have your bedroom, and when you come home, you can't have it back. You'll have to have the room I'm in now. I like your room best. There are hiding spaces. I've seen."

Martha giggled as she watched her sister think. She always knew when Jill was thinking about something because her lips tightened up like a peanut and her eyes met in the middle. Her sister was thinking about what she'd found in her bedroom. She knew it. She'd had a good look through. It served Jill right for going out and eating pickled eggs with the boy. Jill wasn't allowed to see boys. Not after the last time when there was all the shouting, and she had to turn the TV up to hear her show. Then Jill had gone away. Mom and Dad said she couldn't have Jill's bedroom. They wanted everything to be normal again when Jill came back.

"I found it," Martha said. "I looked inside too."

"I don't care," Jill said.

"Mom and Dad will care when I tell them. You're not supposed to eat pickled eggs with boys. When I tell them where to look and they see, you'll go nowhere ever again, not even to university. As punishment, Mom and Dad will give me your bedroom, because it has hiding spaces. Just see if they don't."

Martha saw Jill smiling to herself then, the smile that came on her face when she was going to win at snakes and ladders.

"Whatever you think you saw isn't there," Jill said, "which means it was never there."

Martha scrunched up her hands into two tiny balls of annoyance. She knew Jill wasn't telling a fib. There was something in the way she said there was nothing there now that made her believe there was nothing there. Mom and Dad wouldn't believe her if she told them about what she saw, and then there was nothing there for them to see. They'd think it was another one of her made-up stories about Jill, and she'd told too many made-up stories about Jill in the past for her to be believed. There had to be another way for her to tell all, for her to get Jill's bedroom, where she could play and sleep and never have to see Jill or Mom and Dad again if she didn't want to. There'd be so much space to do so many things in there. If she could think hard enough, she could say something which would mean she'd win snakes and ladders. Then she thought of something.

"The boy isn't gone," Martha said. "I saw him, and I'll see him today at church. I know what he looks like. Then Mom and Dad will know what he looks like. I'll point him out for them to see. Then Mom and Dad will see you, and they'll know that I'm telling the truth. You can't make a pickled egg disappear, like what I found and saw."

Martha watched with satisfaction as she saw Jill's lips again become a peanut and her eyes again meet in the middle. Now it was time for her sister to think hard if she was going to win snakes and ladders. Satisfied with herself, she thought of Uncle Crow. At first, she didn't believe what she'd seen after church the last time. Mom and Dad hadn't seen. Jill hadn't seen. They didn't see the things she saw. She was smaller. There were some things that only small people could see. Only she'd seen Uncle Crow hiding in the trees. Mom had turned all funny when she'd seen her drawing of Uncle Crow, like the way she turned when she changed what show was on the TV when something happened that shouldn't be happening. It wasn't her fault that Uncle Crow looked that way. She'd only drawn and coloured what she'd seen. Uncle Crow had arms and legs, just like people, and a big crow head, not like people. He also wore clothes that people wore when they went to church to bury someone, all black like a crow that was all black, too. Uncle Crow, she'd named him. Something about Uncle Crow made her think he wasn't an auntie.

Ernie

Ernie arrived at the church at the same time he did every Sunday, that moment when half of the people were awake and going about their regularities and the other half were still asleep as though they had nothing to do ever and so what was the point in setting an alarm clock, even on Christmas Day. This morning though, after his wife's long talk with him, he'd had to turn his regular amble into a brisk stride to get to the church on time, and accordingly he now found himself out of breath.

Ernie leaned against Reginald Iver to get his wind back, though not the living Reginald Iver, but the man's weathered gravestone. Reginald Iver had died in 1896 at 81, a good innings by anybody's reckoning, and he was dearly missed by his wife Elizabeth who had passed on a year later and who was now leaning against her husband in her own particular way, the couple's gravestones touch and touching in a loving I'm-with-you-and-you're-with-me manner.

Ernie looked upwards to the sky and the bunches of madly vocalising crows that were flying above him, the blackness of them blotching white with falling snow. "Those crows disturbing your rest, Reggie?"

Ernie enjoyed chatting with the graveyard's permanent residents. It could be lonely work tending the church grounds, and many a person taking a shortcut through the graveyard had seen him talking to the departed, and they'd laugh, or move on faster, or be silent, later thinking perhaps that when they died, they'd like to have to someone like him talking to them after they were in the ground. Whatever the reaction, he didn't mind. It was his opinion that even the dead liked to have someone talking to them, especially when their loved ones only visited them occasionally, if at all.

"Reggie," Ernie said, "my Deirdre is going to be the death of me. I tell you it won't be long before you see me down there with you."

His wife's talk with him lingered on his mind and his bones. Deirdre hadn't minced words in telling him how it was high time he retired, that he shouldn't be working with his heart and all, and especially on Christmas day. She'd said that she didn't want to find out one day that he'd keeled over into a grave he'd been digging for somebody else. "She has a point," Ernie said to Reggie. "I'm not long for this world, and shouldn't I be spending what time I have left with her instead of up here? She'd get me working on those bloody jigsaws she's always doing, so that's something to think about, isn't it? It's the Hanging Gardens of Babylon this week."

Ernie walked over to Margaret Mortimer's gravestone. She'd passed on seven years after Reggie. There had been no-one to write on her stone that she was dearly missed. "Marge, now you're a woman, or you were. Perhaps you'd be able to help me out on this?"

Of course, there wasn't a word out of Margaret.

"Your silence says it all," Ernie said. "It's about time I packed it all in. I don't have to be here, truth be told. We've enough to keep a roof over our heads for the time that we need it with a little left over for a few home comforts. And I could still come and visit, couldn't I? I might even persuade Deirdre to come along with me, but you know how she feels about coming up here. I can't say that I blame her for that."

Ernie thought about the girl he'd seen earlier. What was her name now? Jill, that was it. The boy she'd been waiting for. Now what was his name again? Alex, that was his name. The pair were a few of the Church Ones left, dragged along by their families. He supposed that their time at the church was only made bearable because they got to see each other, never speaking, but seeing. He'd see them both this morning, sure enough. It wasn't what the two of them had planned.

"What was that you said, Victoria?" Ernie asked. He walked over to Victoria Thomas's grave. "Now what's got you turning over down there this time."

Of course, there wasn't a word out of Victoria.

"I hear them too." Ernie said, looking up at the crows, "There's something brewing around here and it's not a good pot of tea." An empty crisp packet blew onto Victoria's grave. He bent over to pick it up. As he did, his bones creaked and ached. It might've been the weather, Deirdre's talking to him, or the crows, but today he felt like he had only one dug grave left in his body. It would be a pity. There wasn't a soul who could quite work a shovel into the ground the way he could, he was sure of it. Deirdre was right. He should get out while he still could, on his own two feet, before he keeled over. He'd make good on having to work today. Then he'd stop in the church to tell the new vicar his decision.

Ernie looked up to the church and there he saw the new vicar march outside and throw something away that looked like a black dish rag, but wasn't that at all, among the gravestones. "Oh my, Victoria. Oh, my."

His employer caught sight of him. "What are you looking at? Get back to work! Mrs Robertson will be here tomorrow, and she'll want her grave dug!"

Ernie watched the new vicar hurry back into the church.

"If you'll excuse me," Ernie said, patting Victoria's gravestone, "I'm needed elsewhere."

Ernie strode over to where the dead crow had landed, halfway between the six-feet-under Hingle sisters, as he did so he couldn't help but notice on the way all the small things that needed to be taken care of, put right, which no one would probably ever notice once he'd walked away from his job. He knelt down in front of the mutilated crow. "You poor thing."

He'd spoken to the police about the new vicar, about what had gone on. He'd told them he'd seen nothing, which was true, and that he knew of nothing, which was false, because what would they have thought of him when he told them he could see the stories in people? The police would have laughed at him. They may've even locked him up instead. Now, though, he had seen and knew of something that could be told. The same went for the crows high above him, louder and louder, as though they were calling the world to an end. He took up the crow for Mrs Robertson to have a neighbour.

Oliver

Oliver had parked his car at the bottom of the hill that led up to the church. After the long drive from Manchester, he was glad of the chance to stretch his legs, despite having to watch his step on the snow-slippy pavement. Halfway up the hill, he felt somewhat like his old self. His breath caught the air and materialised into white and wispy ghosts about his face, haunting him as he went.

In the course of his work for the diocese, Oliver had never travelled to Birmingham. Now here he was and early enough to peruse the outside of the church before carrying out his work. Already, he could glimpse hints of the church's attractive stone decoration between branches of oak and sycamore, stoking a fire inside of him that succeeded for a moment in chasing away the cold of the day. It would be a pleasure to take a few photos of the church for his album. What a pity his superiors had written into their bad books such architectural splendour. They'd sent a letter, of course. Now they'd sent him. A church inspector always followed a letter.

"Oi, you," said one of two young boys walking down the hill towards Oliver. The boy wore only a t-shirt despite the worsening weather.

"Ain't goin' up to church?" the other boy asked, sporting a claret and blue bruise over his right eye.

The two kids stopped a couple of feet in front of Oliver, fencing off his way up to the church.

"Morning," Oliver said.

"You look like one of those who'd be going up there," the t-shirt boy said.

Oliver took infinite care to dress as though he'd fit into any Sunday morning congregation up and down the country. His face, for that matter, benefited his work too. On being hired for the position of church inspector, he'd been told that he'd the perfect face for the work, a face that blended into the surroundings so that it may as well not be there at all. Nobody would ever know what he was doing there, it was agreeably said, or if he'd been there at all.

"You don't think I should go?" Oliver asked. He'd studied the file the diocese had sent him about the church, but a file was just a file. One could only get to know more about what was truly going on by turning up yourself, by watching and listening and talking to the locals. That was the job of a church inspector.

"Be your funeral if you do," the bruised eye boy said.

"Then maybe you'd like to tell me more," Oliver said.

"If you were from around here, you'd know," the t-shirt boy said.

"Something about the vicar?" Oliver asked.

The boys fell silent.

Oliver had spent seven years as a church inspector, and he knew that sometimes you had to give a little something to get a little something back. "How about five pounds for everything you know?"

Oliver watched as the bruised eye boy whispered something to the t-shirt boy.

“Make it a tenner,” the t-shirt boy said, his voice scratchy and phlegmy as though he wouldn’t be long for a doctor’s visit.

“Fair enough,” Oscar said, taking out his wallet, opening it up, paying no mind to the t-shirt boy whispering to the bruised eye boy.

The two boys were quickly upon Oliver, catching him off-guard, pushing him so that he slipped on the snowy pavement, slapping flat on his back. The fall knocked all the wind from his body and he lay on the pavement without the function within him to move. He looked up at the two boys through the falling snow, who looked down at him. Then they were about and into his body, fast and practised, their bones like sharpened little knives.

When they were done with him, Oliver heard the two boys laughing and skittering away, down and down the hill. He knew they wouldn’t slip and fall. He knew that he’d never catch up. Far away now, he was certain too that he heard the t-shirt boy with his sickbed voice call out, “Be your funeral!”

May

May wrangled Ida, Doris, and Betty through the swinging iron gate and into the church grounds. "Get a move on," she said. "It's really coming down now."

"Look at the crows," Ida said.

"I'm looking, and it's giving me the willies," Doris said.

"It's like what I read in my horoscope," Betty said.

May slapped together her gloved hands to generate some warmth for herself. "Never mind that, let's get out of this snow."

Each Sunday, May would take to church those from the home that wanted to go. That number had dwindled quickly after the first occasion they'd tried out the new vicar. After that service, most of the home's residents had returned saying that was enough church for them, and that they didn't need that sort of thing in their lives, and that they'd rather eat Cook's Tuesday night liver and onions. Not so Ida, Doris, and Betty.

May walked behind the three octogenarians, telling them every now and again to watch their step. She had it within her to think that they weren't long for the world. They'd drop off soon enough, and then she wouldn't have to sit through the new vicar. The others were right, even a plate of Cook's Tuesday night liver and onions was better than being stuck in a pew listening to the church's windbag. The old vicar? Now he'd been a Christmas dinner to eat up. She hadn't minded him taking up her time.

"Watch that icy part coming up," May said, noticing their path up to the church taking a turn for the worse.

"We see it," Ida said.

"We can look and walk too," Doris said.

"Beware the colour black. It warned me," Betty said. "I thought it was about my jumper. I was going to put on my black one. That's why I'm wearing my green one. Now I know it meant these crows all along."

May looked at her watch and saw that there were still fifteen minutes to kick off. Shouldn't she be hearing the church bells ringing by now? Not these crows that wouldn't shut up in the same fashion that Ida, Doris, and Betty wouldn't shut up. Surely she could find a better job than this one? She'd heard about an opening coming up at the Heart Foundation Shop. She'd have to pop down there on Monday and inquire. Having been a carer all of her life, and if the truth be told, she'd stop caring about her career, such as it was, a long time ago. That had snowballed into her not caring too much about herself, either. Still, despite all of that, she had a job to do. Yes, Ida, Doris, Betty ran up headaches in her, the splitting kind that made her want to poke her eyes out with one of Doris' knitting needles, but when all was said and done, they weren't a bad bunch. If she ever reached their age, she wouldn't mind being cut from the same woolly cloth. They certainly still had a life about them while they were knocking on Death's door.

"Ooh look, there's Ernie," Ida said. "Doesn't he dig a lovely grave?"

"I hope he's around to do mine when my time comes," Doris said.

"You can tell a lot about a man in how he handles a shovel," Betty said.

Ida, Doris, and Betty waved at Ernie.

Ernie waved back.

May waved too, as she did every Sunday. She'd never spoken to the man, as he was always too many gravestones removed, but he had one of those kinds of faces that was instantly likeable, a face you wanted to wave at to say hello. Why he was still doing his kind of work at his age was beyond her, though. In this weather, too. And on Christmas Day. By her accounting, today he looked as though he was ready to fall down into the hole he was digging.

"A murder, that's what they call it," Ida said. "A murder of crows."

"There's only one murderer up here," Doris said.

"Beware the colour black," Betty said. "It was in my horoscope, and I always go by my horoscope. It wasn't my jumper, it was these crows."

"Well, the sooner we get inside, the sooner we won't have to be bothered by them," May said, placing a hurry-along hand on Betty's shoulder.

Betty took to her walking stick as though she were a conductor at the part of the piece of music when all the instruments pipe into battle at once. "There's one on me!"

May dodged an approaching blow. "It's only me, Betty!"

Betty opened her eyes that she'd shut tight in her supposed crow attack. "Don't sneak up on me like that! I may be old, but I can still do some damage, crow or you!"

"Can we all keep focused, and do what we came here to do," May said, "or I'll have to write all three of you up for causing a nuisance."

Ida, Doris, and Betty pottered on.

"Why you all still come here is beyond me," May said.

"We're putting a case together," Ida said.

"The police couldn't solve it, but we are," Doris said.

"You wouldn't think there'd be so many crows, and then they all come out and there they are," Betty said.

This was a new one, thought May. "What case?"

"We'll be in the papers," Ida said.

"Make it The Mirror for me," Doris said. "That's a good read."

"The day my Fred died, I told him he shouldn't be going down the pub," Betty said. "My horoscope said my nearest and dearest should stay at home. As Lily had just passed on, that left Fred as my nearest and dearest. Don't go down the pub, I told him. But did he listen? No! And what happened? Well, leaving and drunk to high heaven, he fell down into the pub's barrel cellar. His pal that was with him, Eric, said he fell through the hole singing that song 'Tiger Feet.' He always liked Mud, the silly bugger."

"Today's the day," Ida said. "It came to us over our hot chocolates, didn't it girls? The last piece of the puzzle that'll put him away."

"Let's not get ahead of ourselves," Doris said.

"Today's the day all right," Betty said. "We're all done for today. Beware the colour black, I read. My horoscope is never wrong. I thought it was about my black jumper, but we can all see now."

May didn't have a clue what case Ida and Doris were going on about. They were always going off into the land of the loopy, but Betty's ramblings about her horoscope and the crows were getting to her. "Now Betty, there's nothing to worry about," she said. "It's just a regular day."

Though having said that, May walked closer to Ida, Doris, and Betty. Out of protection for them or herself, she didn't quite know. As they went, she noticed that the new vicar wasn't looming, as usual, Grim Reaper-like at the church door, waiting for arrivals. Crows weren't the only ones to dress in black. A vicar did too. May stopped that line of thinking abruptly. Betty had well and truly got into her head. Thankfully, inside of the church, Betty would forget about the crows, which would mean she could, too. If all was right with the world, the crows would have gone when they came back out, back to wherever they came from.

Martha

Together they sat on a bench tucked back among gravestones.

"I ran out of black doing it. Black is my favourite colour. I always run out of black first." Martha said. "Do you like it?"

Uncle Crow nodded his big crow's head.

Martha smiled, knowing that Uncle Crow liked her drawing of him, not like Mom. "You know, you're kind of scary-looking."

Again, Uncle Crow nodded his big crow's head.

"But I'm not scared," Martha said.

Uncle Crow patted Martha on the head.

"You can keep it," Martha said.

Uncle Crow placed Martha's drawing, the paper now sodden and flimsy from the snow, inside of his big crow's head beak.

"Do you like licorice?" Martha asked.

Once more, Uncle Crow nodded his big crow's head.

"Licorice is black too. Mom and Dad and Jill don't like licorice, so I don't have to share. Jill should like licorice, because she has licorice hair. I wish I had licorice hair like Jill has. Mom says I have to make do, but I don't want to make do. One night when Jill was asleep, I cut some of her hair for myself. She doesn't know. Don't tell, okay?"

Martha liked the way Uncle Crow chuckled when she'd said what she said. It was the sound of lots of crows inside of him where she couldn't see.

"Mom and Dad and Jill will be angry I'm gone," Martha said.

Uncle Crow nodded his big crow's head.

Martha didn't want to be with Mom and Dad and Jill. She wanted to be with Uncle Crow. Mom and Dad and Jill were flies on a bun with her. She'd seen flies on a bun. Mom and Dad and Jill were the flies, and she was the bun. She'd escaped the flies. It had been easy with her mom and dad arguing with the boy's dad and with all the snow. She wasn't a bun with flies all over with Uncle Crow.

Uncle Crow stood up.

Martha stood up too, as it seemed the thing to do. Uncle Crow was far up in the sky taller than her. She'd nearly run out of paper drawing him. She watched with fascination as Uncle Crow took a long and thin musical instrument from out of himself, one that looked like the vacuum attachment her Mom used when she wanted to sweep up the places that never got swept because they were hiding, and then put the musical instrument to his big crow's head beak and played.

Martha had never heard music like Uncle Crow's music. It wasn't like the music that came out of Mom's and Dad's record player. Neither was it like the music that came out of Jill's phone. And it wasn't like the music that came out of the TV when she turned it on to watch one of her shows. Uncle Crows's music made her feel funny in her insides, like the times she didn't have to go to school because she felt funny in her insides. Perhaps she wouldn't have to go to church today? That would make her happy, as she didn't want to go to church today. She wanted to stay with Uncle Crow, feeling funny in her insides. She looked upwards to the sky, where Uncle Crow was looking while he played his music. The crows that she saw there looked to her as though all of them were feeling funny in their insides, too. The crows that she saw there looked like they were multiplying from out of a sum she didn't understand.

"You're the best Christmas present, Uncle Crow," Martha said.

On hearing this, and perhaps to celebrate, Uncle Crow danced.

Martha danced too, as it seemed like the thing to do. Although she'd never danced Uncle Crow's dance before, she knew the dance off by heart, better than she knew anything she could think of. And she liked the dance, even feeling funny in her insides. It was a feeling funny in her insides kind of dance.

Crow

It was something.

Now it is nothing.

We tell each other this.

We see.

It should not be.

That is the word.

The word is spreading.

We know of other times.

Our memories are with us.

They can be again.

That is the word.

Alex

Alex grabbed Jill by the hand and pulled her away from her family and into the safety of the church's vestibule. Behind him, he could hear his father yelling at him, and Jill's family yelling at him, and all of them behaving as though the crows swooping down upon them, fast and many, from out of the snowy sky were nothing but a mere distraction when compared to their arguments over him and Jill.

Alex pulled Jill close. They held each other, cold and wet with melting snow. "I was going to be there."

"You're here now," Jill said.

Alex parted from Jill to look at her. It wasn't the day they'd planned, but now they were together again. When they were together, everything was all right, even when, really, everything wasn't all right.

"You're bleeding," Alex said, seeing that a crow had scratched Jill across her forehead, a scratch that would probably need stitches.

Jill tugged Alex's hand. "Let's go now, just go, okay?"

Alex had never seen Jill look at him the way she was looking at him now. He'd never seen her eyes so desperate.

"We can't," Alex said.

"It's not safe here," Jill said.

"It's safer than out there."

"Not when they come in."

"The crows?"

"No, our families, silly."

A commotion grew inside of the church, and Alex saw the faces of people he knew and didn't know, all of their faces a different artist's brush strokes of what it may be like to fall into a sudden hell.

Alex grasped Jill's hand.

Jill shook Alex away. "Where's Martha?"

Alex looked about, down from the high places and into the low places where little Martha would be. He couldn't see her. There, though, was Jill going to her family asking for Martha, and he could see that they didn't know. He could also see his father approaching him. Then he was going from his father, going from Jill and her family, going from an appearing spectre of a man dressed in black, and he was going and going to look for Martha. He heard a mighty thud behind him, the sound of a great door closing as though it would never open again. He didn't look back.

Outside, the sky was white, and the sky was black, and the white and the black came down upon Alex and the white and the black was a cold and a hot pain and a noise shrouding and snuffing out his calls for Martha. Jill had often spoken of her sister, and she'd spoken about her in a good way and she'd spoken about her in a bad way. He hadn't been there for Jill, but somewhere Martha waited, like Jill had waited, and he could be there for Martha, couldn't he?

Through the church's graveyard, Alex ran, flinging his arms about to keep the crows at bay, a windmill off its hinges. Through the heavy snowfall, he saw a person, and then he didn't, and then he did, the wind catching the snow and it making it a curtain for his eyes, parting and then drawing. It couldn't be Martha. The person he saw and then didn't see was in the high places and Martha would be in the low places. Then the person he didn't see and then saw fell from the high places and down into the low places where Martha would be. It couldn't have been Martha. The curtain parted again and there was the person and there were the crows. The person cast out an arm to him for him to come, and then the curtain was drawn on him again and the crows that were there too. He was glad of it because he hadn't wanted to see it. He was glad that it wasn't Martha.

Martha

Martha looked down from the high places to the low places, and there she saw a fly coming for her and calling her name, regular as clockwork, tick-tock. Through the falling snow, now she saw the fly, and then she didn't see the fly. The fly was Jill's boy who'd tried to run away with Jill while Mom and Dad weren't looking. She'd run away while Mom and Dad and Jill weren't looking to be with Uncle Crow. Now the fly was coming for her, to run away with her while Uncle Crow wasn't looking. She wanted to stay with Uncle Crow. The fly could shoo, shoo away without her. She belonged to Uncle Crow.

Then she belonged to the fly. She couldn't stop it. She was in the low places and the fly was in the high places, all over her, a fly on a bun, taking her away, far from Uncle Crow away. Uncle Crow didn't see it happening. She then fell behind a curtain with the fly. She'd never eat pickled eggs ever. Never. One day, she'd be in the high places. Then it would be different. She missed Uncle Crow already.

Ernie

All Ernie could think about was what Deirdre would say if she could see the pickle he'd got himself into this time. She'd likely tell him, I told you. I said no good would come of you working up there. And on Christmas Day too, the shame of it. Now look at you. Good grief, now look at me! What am I supposed to do now you're going to be off? What do you have to say for yourself? Speak up! Don't just lay there dying like that!

Of course, Deirdre would've every right to put on one of her faces and flounce into a fit. He'd keep on thinking about Deirdre. It helped park the horror of the pain a little to the side. Making Christmas dinner, that's what Deirdre would be up to there in the kitchen. She could never make proper Yorkshire pudding, bless her. He should be at home putting her straight on matters rather than becoming bits and pieces, much like the bits and pieces of potato that were Deirdre's mash. She could never make proper mashed potatoes either, bless her.

He had a plot back near the blackberry bushes with Deirdre's place, when it was her time, beside him. They'd have to move him up there from where he was now. Who'd dig a dead gravedigger's grave? The old vicar had bought the plots for Deirdre and him saying nobody else picks the blackberries there but you, so I thought it would be the very spot. It was perhaps the best birthday present he'd ever received. That and the tool kit Deirdre had bought him for his fortieth. Who'd use those tools now? It wasn't like Deirdre liked to mess about with fixing things, bless her. That's why she'd brought him the tool kit, and a good one it was too. It must've taken all the year for her to save up for, bless her. He'd been making Deirdre a new bread box for her birthday. She couldn't make proper Yorkshire pudding or proper mashed potatoes, but she had a way of making a loaf that would put any baker to shame, bless her. Now Deirdre would walk into the garden shed and look at a lot of wood laying about, and she'd probably say, What was the old food up to in here? I've no idea! She'd never know he'd been making a bread box for her birthday.

He wondered who'd tell Deirdre about what had happened? He hoped it wouldn't be the new vicar. If he turned up on Deirdre's doorstep, he'd better be ready for a shakeup. He'd think he knocked on the very Devil's door. He knew his Deirdre. She'd be making a blackberry and apple crumble for afters with the blackberries that were picked and then frozen for eating when the blackberry bushes were nothing but thorny skeletons. Deirdre had a way with a crumble too, bless her. Would she come up and visit him in blackberry season and have a natter about what was going on and then pick some blackberries to take back home and make a crumble? He hoped so. Deirdre liked her blackberry crumble with custard. He was one for having it without. He couldn't see the snow now that his eyes were gone, but he knew it was covering him over like custard over Deirdre's bowl of crumble.

He'd fallen over Lulu when the crows came for him, and then it had already been too late to get up. The crows wouldn't allow it. Lulu was a funny name. He supposed she'd been named after the singer. She'd passed on at 39. He'd be 76. His mother had named him Earnest after a character in a play. That was a funny name, too. His father had wanted nothing to do with the idea. It was his mother that wanted to name him Earnest. His father had called him Ernie. He didn't mind either way. Sometimes Deirdre would call him Earnest, but only when he was up for a good telling off. Other times it would be plain old Ernie. Everybody down the pub called him Ernie. He wouldn't make the dominoes tournament Saturday coming. That'd be a pity. He felt like he was in with a chance of winning now that Willie had passed on. Willie was down by the oak tree. He'd been 83. Lulu was 39. Ray was 18. Harriet was 59. Peter was six months old, bless him. Rita was 24. Diedre still had a few good years in her before she was up by the blackberry bushes with him, bless her. He'd heard someone, and they'd seen him. It was the boy, Alex, but then he couldn't see the boy, and he supposed the boy couldn't see him. The boy couldn't have helped, anyway. There was a story in the boy, and he wasn't written into it. He'd the eyes to see for a moment. He heard music too, but it wasn't the type of heavenly music he'd been told to expect. He'd be 76 in Mrs Robertson's grave. They'd have to move him before she arrived tomorrow. Up by the blackberry bushes.

Archibald

After Archibald had flatly refused to open the large wooden doors of the church, brandishing the spiked skull of The Reverend Stephen Watts, the head of the church's third vicar having being severed and put on the spike as a warning to those that had leanings of Catholicism over the state religion, to clarify with everyone that he truly meant business, he'd counted his congregation. It was a lower number than the previous week, but there were three new faces. Why they were all behaving as though their hands had traded places with their feet without them knowing was beyond him. His sermon would knock some sense into their heads.

It would be a closed door performance. To help with that, he'd phoned the organist, to let her know she wouldn't be needed. She'd said over the phone, "I've been practising a new piece all week!" He'd wanted to tell her she could practise for a lifetime, but she'd still be a living crime to musicianship. Instead, he'd said she could enjoy the morning off with the butcher. That had shut her up. As for the choirmaster, he'd relaxed into having the day off quickly. There was only one left in the choir and that was his butterball son, who couldn't hit the note of a hymn with a long run up and a cricket bat. The choirmaster had asked him if he'd been drinking. He'd replied that yes, he was drunk with the Lord, and that the choirmaster would do himself good to follow suit. For the rest of his staff, the assistant curate, the parish administrator, the churchwarden, the verger, the readers, and the rest, they'd stopped coming months ago. He hadn't told the diocese about that, of course. It was probably one of them that had written to the diocese about him, bringing about the diocese's letter to him. If he ever got his hands on the person who blabbed, they'd get the same treatment as the old vicar. They'd lumbered him with a motley crew of amateurs, incompetents, and taletellers to work with from the start, alright. Was it any wonder he and his church had come under scrutiny!

Archibald looked upon his congregation and, on seeing what he had to work with, knew that he'd once again be attempting to fashion a silk purse out of a sow's ear. The state of them, as though they'd dragged themselves through the bushes backwards! That and they were all babbling something or other about crows. Frankly, he'd had enough of crows for the day. He wished they'd all put a cork in it. They were making it difficult for him to keep his sermon between his ears.

"Take your seats, we haven't got all day," Archibald said to one and all, holding aloft the church's rare and gruesome artefact, the Reverend Stephen Watts' skull rattling atop the spike as if it too would have something to say about matters if order wasn't restored promptly. The congregation quieted from shouts to mutters. With that, he heard a banging on the church door. What now? He hated late arrivals. Still, how many more than those already gathered would hear him today? He supposed he could open the door to give shelter to those that asked this one occasion.

Jack

Jack yanked Alex to the pews and there pressed his son down into a seat next to him. He said to Alex, "Run from me one more time, do you hear me?" He left it at that, folding Alex's hand into his hand to make Alex's hand his hand too. The vicar had told them to sit down, but the others weren't listening. He'd listened. His son would listen.

Jack saw the girl that had his son wrapped around her little finger. She wasn't listening. He knew her type. You only had to look at her to see that she was a troublemaker. His wife had been a troublemaker. He'd soon put a stop to that. He'd do the same with the girl soon enough, or sooner. The others too, if they carried on as the girl was carrying on. The new vicar was speaking. They should all be listening. They could see him. His son's hand was now his hand. There'd be no running. Together they'd listen, and together they'd see. They weren't the others. They wanted to run. Three of them already were. Most would see two people, but he saw three. The man was around the woman. He was once around his wife that way when Alex was inside of her. The new vicar wanted the three to stay, and he sent out his voice as a wall to be put down in front of them, but a wall was no match for a man around a woman that way. Good riddance. He knew the others wanted to follow, but they couldn't because of the blackness coming in, stopping them. They were too late for running.

He'd once heard the same screams when he was working across from a man, and the man got pulled in and was eaten up. The man had screamed as though his whole family had been inside of him. He'd heard the man's screaming and his wife's screaming and his daughter's screaming. They'd all died that day, not just the man. He was asked if there'd been anything he could've done to stop it. He could've done something, but he hadn't said that. He'd said his eyes had been on the job. He'd said it'd been too late before he saw what was going on. They were taught to keep their eyes on the job. They got pulled in and eaten up if their eyes weren't on the job. They got fired if their eyes weren't on the job. He'd got away with it. He didn't say his eyes weren't on the job. He didn't say he wasn't working. He didn't say he saw it all, and could've done something. It'd been better than the tele, seeing the man get pulled in and eaten up, hearing the screams of the man and his wife and his daughter. The man's eyes should've been on the job and then he wouldn't have got pulled in and eaten up.

His son would sit and listen and see with him. If the blackness pulled them in and ate them up, so be it. His screams would be in his son's screams, and his son's screams would be in his screams. He knew all about the blackness. His father had worked in a coal mine and had said that not even the closet under the stairs without the light where his father put him when he'd been up to no good was as black as down the coal mine. His father said that even with a light, you knew the blackness walked with you, hiding, and could take you away so that you wouldn't be found for all the looking. His father said the blackness didn't like to hide for long, the blackness liked to come out and say I'm here now. You couldn't find me, but I found you. The blackness coming in was the same blackness of his father coming up from the coal mine, taking up the new vicar and carrying him high, coming for all of them. He'd watch. His son would watch too.

Jill

They threaded a family line of Dad, Martha, Mom, and then finally her, each of them holding the other's hand, her dad leading the way out of the church. At school, Ms Smith used to march her friends and her through the playground in the same way. They were to stay together, not letting go of hands, Ms Smith had said. They were to stay together, not letting go of hands, her dad had said.

Jill looked behind her and saw Alex, held down by his father, falling deeper into his father, unable to move, a headstone. They weren't leaving. She willed her hand to be air slipping through her mom's hand for her to go to Alex. She let go of her mom's hand. She wasn't to let go, her dad had said, but she let go, her hand had been air. As her family went from her, not letting go of each other, she saw one, two, three, four, five crows upon them. Her family was three, the crows were five. She'd let go. There was nothing she could do to help her family, but she had it within her to help Alex deep within his father. She'd been down to the places Alex went to find him before, and she'd brought him back up to her. She hurried to Alex, and her family hurried from her, her hand had been air, her mom wouldn't be to blame.

Jill once saw her mom's black blouse blown from off the washing line by the wind and then away and across the street to wrap around a man's face. That was the crow and Alex's father together. She didn't want to see. She looked away. She knelt down in front of Alex, unable to move, held by his father. Martha had once asked her to pull her up into the night sky, and she'd held out her hand, and she'd put her hand into Martha's hand, and she'd pulled her sister up into the night sky. They'd been lying on Martha's bed, looking up at the ceiling where there were stars and planets put there to see. Martha had told her to never let go of her hand, that she never wanted to come back down. She'd let go of Martha's hand. She'd let go of her mother's hand. She took Alex's free hand in hers. She wouldn't let go. Alex's eyes were blue, but they were black. Her eyes were stars and planets.

May

May wished Ida, Doris, and Berry would get a move on. She knew they could hurry along when they wanted. She'd seen them racing for a table when it was burger and chips night back at home.

"Mind the head of our Lord," Ida said.

"I don't want to look at it," Doris said.

"We'll be in the papers tomorrow," Betty said.

May pushed Ida, Doris, and Betty along. "Never mind all that."

May swung at a crow that had taken a liking to Ida, successfully frightening the bird away. While she did that, another crow took a liking to her, and she gave that bird some of the same. If she'd been born with any sense, she would carry on as fast as the others were carrying on, forgetting the old dears to save herself.

"The new vicar knows we're onto him," Ida said.

"There were eyes moving in our Lord's head," Doris said.

"We'll be on the tele too, not just in the papers," Betty said.

It came to May that if she were to leave Ida, Doris, and Betty behind, they'd likely come back to haunt her. They were just the type.

"You left us," Ida's ghost would say.

"We came back," Doris's ghost would say.

"Put the kettle on," Betty's ghost would say. "We're staying for a bit."

May regretted the day she'd got into healthcare. There'd be no coming back to the church after this. She'd see to that. Then come Monday, she'd see about the job at the charity shop. She wouldn't have to work Sundays. They were closed on Sundays, and she wouldn't have the worry of escaping a working day with her life intact.

"I saw a robin the other day," Ida said. "They're my favourite. It was a robin you like to see on a Christmas card, one you'd want to send to somebody you like. You don't have this kind of to-do with robins."

"I hope the cook roasts the sprouts for our dinner," Doris said. "He knows we don't like it when he boils them. Like eating green mush, it is."

"I'll take his boiled sprouts over his liver and onions any day of the week," Betty said.

Talk of Christmas Day dinner put May on her sofa at home eating alone. Her mom had been calling her to come over. She'd run out of excuses for why it wasn't a good time this time this year. Her mom cooked the best Christmas dinner with all the trimmings, just the way she liked it. She did care for her mom, though she never said as much. She wanted to say as much. She'd like her mom to know that she cared. Once, after they'd watched the movie with the shark together, she'd had to sit on the edge of the bathtub reading the paper while her mom took a bath because a shark might've come up through the plug hole. She'd cared then. Her mom had known she'd cared then. Betty was right, they'd all be in the papers tomorrow, on the tele too. Her mom would read about it, see it, and she'd have to eat her Christmas dinner alone again, without her.

"One of 'em took my hat," Ida said. "My George gave me that hat."

"It's a horrible hat," Doris said. "You should be grateful."

"Look, it's up as high as the new vicar." Betty said. "They've got him bang to rights up there and no mistake. My horoscope is never wrong."

May kept Ida, Dorris, and Betty going, as to see again what she'd seen above her would surely have been enough for her eyes to give up on her.

Derek and Carol

Derek lay next to Carol, who lay next to something opened up, small and red and raw. The snow was a rolled out blanket for the three of them.

Archibald

Archibald could hear sirens. The sirens would be too late for him. He'd be gone. There'd been sirens for the old vicar that were too late for him. He'd been gone, too. He'd got away with it. While they, the crows, held him in the high places, crucified in the air, like his Lord once was, in tatters and shreds, he'd taken satisfaction that in death people would remember him as they'd never done in life. People would pass his name down from generation to generation. They would talk about him in their homes, in the pubs, and queuing up to carry on their humdrum existence. He'd be a bedtime story to frighten both children and adults alike. He'd haunt the town, its people, and the church until kingdom come. Damn the letter to hell. This time next week, the church would be a full house, packed to the heavens, for that Sunday and all the Sundays after. They could bring out a puppet dressed up as a vicar and it wouldn't make a difference to the church's takings. It would be all his doing. A turnaround, a resurrection, which would've put the old vicar to shame. They could all run from him today, but they'd all come running back. One of them hasn't run, the fool. One of the new faces. He can't lift me up. They, the crows, were on him, like the crows had been on him. Serves him right. There, off he goes. A very merry Christmas for you! His father had a good Welsh singing voice. He could hear his father singing now. There were other voices singing with his father. They weren't an angelic choir. His father had been a wicked man. His father's hand was taking him under before the others could put him under. He'd be back. This was his church and it wouldn't be taken away from him, not on this or any other day.

Oliver

He'd tried to help the new vicar, but he was having none of it. What could he have done? The man was a jigsaw puzzle with most of the pieces missing. He'd never be put back together. His superiors wouldn't believe his filed report. Oliver, they'd ask him, have you been feeling all right? Are you in need of a lie down? He'd have to agree with them. He had to be in Cornwall tomorrow, though. Birmingham today. Cornwall tomorrow, god willing. There was tomfoolery going on in Lostwithiell, by all accounts. His superiors had sent a letter. He went to where the letters went. That was his job. Perhaps there'd be church photos to be taken that would be worthy of a place in his album?

Crow

New memories are with us.
They dance.
As we danced.
Those that were nothing were with us.
Called to us.
And they danced.
They told us of their times.
We told them of ours.
We were many.
We were together.
The long bones took one of us.
It was nothing.
It became something.
We were together again.
We were a family.
Now we are mourning.
What was something again.
Is now nothing again.
We remember.
We are full.

Alex

Hand in hand, Alex let Jill run him through the churchyard. She'd been going. She'd come back. She brought him up. She hadn't left him there. She hadn't let go. He'd left Jill there, waiting for him. They would've gone already if he hadn't left her there. They were going now, together, hand in glove.

"Don't look behind you," Jill said.

Alex heard the words come out of Jill as though they were words for her to listen to, not for him to listen to. He saw Jill look behind herself. He knew it was harder for Jill not to do that. There were people calling her name. There was no one calling his name. Then he saw Jill look ahead of herself, and for a moment he saw her mom and dad and sister in her eyes. Then her family was gone, her eyes washed blank by tears. He'd never seen Jill cry. He didn't want to see Jill cry ever again. He knew she would.

Alex looked behind himself. Jill had told him not to, but they were words for her, not for him. Jill had been right. He shouldn't have looked. If he hadn't looked, he wouldn't have seen. There was the spectre of his father, reaching out for him, two black pits where his eyes once were, a crow dining from out of the top of his head—his consequence. He told himself he'd be free of his father one day. He knew he wouldn't.

"This is us now," Jill said.

Hand in hand, Alex let Jill run them from out of the churchyard, and the faster they ran, the more they were going. There are always trains, Jill had said. Trains to take them anywhere they wanted to go, regular as clockwork, tick-tock. Weren't there?

End

Born in Birmingham, England, Daz Eek now lives and writes in Down East Maine, the United States.

Join Daz Eek's newsletter for news on future book releases at https://dazeek.blog/.

www.ingramcontent.com/pod-product-compliance
Lightning Source LLC
LaVergne TN
LVHW041133150826
845673LV00007B/2302

* 9 7 9 8 2 2 4 1 4 5 3 5 5 *